The
Last Pair
of
Shoes

With love and gratitude
to my dear parents
Rabbi Faivel and Tzipora Rimler
—S.F.

In honor of Shalva—though he may never know it—an elderly shoemaker from the old country
who sits with pride at the end of a road in a small Israeli town, repairing shoes to last forever.

THE LAST PAIR OF SHOES

Published and Copyrighted © 2005
by
MERKOS L'INYONEI CHINUCH, INC.
770 Eastern Parkway • Brooklyn, New York 11213
(718) 774-4000 • FAX (718) 774-2718

Order Department:
291 Kingston Avenue • Brooklyn, New York 11213
(718) 778-0226 • FAX (718) 778-4148
www.kehotonline.com

ISBN 0-8266-0031-X

Printed in China

by Sashi Fridman
illustrated by Seva

The Last Pair of Shoes

Shalva is an old shoemaker. Rain or shine, you can find him sitting at the edge of the small town where he lives. He is poor and doesn't have his own little shop. All he has is a small wooden table with a few very old tools, but he is the best shoemaker there is.

Once, when the weather was bad and business was slow, I stopped by to say hello.

"Ah!" Shalva greeted me happily, wiping his big, stained hands on a dirty oilcloth.

"You are in no hurry?" he asked me.

"No, not at all!" I answered.

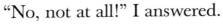

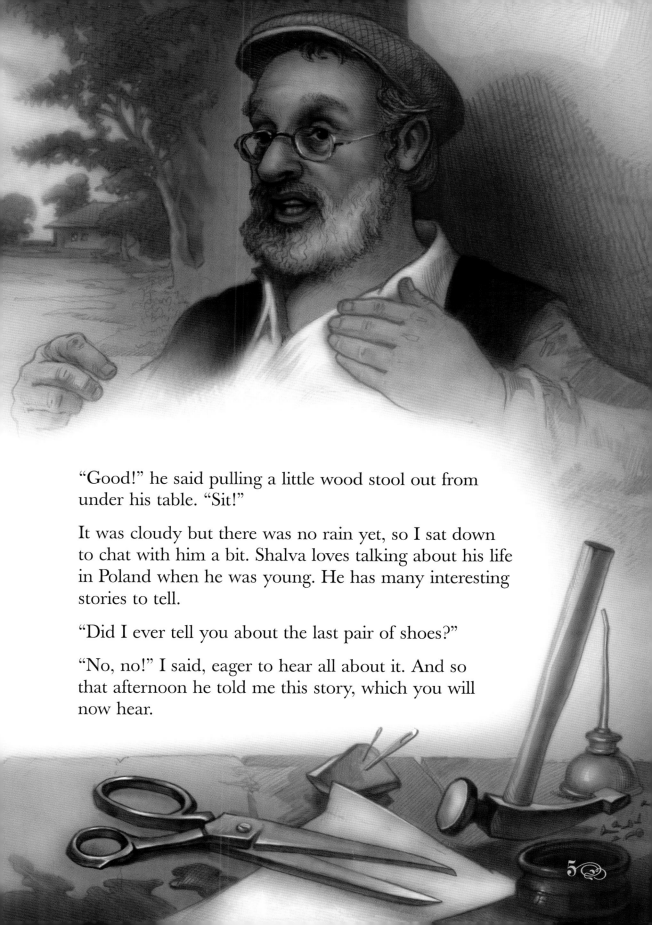

"Good!" he said pulling a little wood stool out from under his table. "Sit!"

It was cloudy but there was no rain yet, so I sat down to chat with him a bit. Shalva loves talking about his life in Poland when he was young. He has many interesting stories to tell.

"Did I ever tell you about the last pair of shoes?"

"No, no!" I said, eager to hear all about it. And so that afternoon he told me this story, which you will now hear.

It was during the war and Shalva's father had gone off to fight.

Shalva was the oldest of six children. Times were hard and there was barely any food. There was almost nothing to be found in the market and only those who could pay a high price were lucky to get some flour. For months they had been unable to even get any sugar!

Yes, it was an unhappy time. The children didn't know the taste of something sweet. They woke up hungry and went to bed hungry, dreaming of food.

Shalva's mother had to take care of the little children, and so Shalva, being the eldest, went out to work.

Before the war, Shalva's father had been a shoemaker.
Young Shalva could always be found in his father's

little shop, watching how his father cut and sewed and hammered away until he produced a fine pair of shoes.

9

So with his father away, Shalva went into the shop and tried to make shoes himself. He had everything he needed: sheets of leather and rubber, wooden pegs and spools of thread.

He worked for many long weeks, until one day he came running home excitedly with a new pair of shoes in his hands.

"Look Mama!" he cried with joy. "I've made a pair of shoes just like Father!"

The children squealed with delight and Shalva's mother clapped her hands and sighed, "Thank G-d! Thank G-d! We shall now be able to buy some flour!"

Shalva sold the shoes and with the money he bought a small sack of flour. For the first time in many weeks the children had some bread and didn't go to sleep hungry. From then on Shalva worked all day and late into the night making shoes.

One morning, Shalva came into the shop and noticed that there was only enough leather left to make one more pair of shoes. The war was dragging on and there was no way he would be able to get more materials to make shoes. "Oh," he thought sadly, "soon I will have to search for other work so that we will not go hungry again."

Shalva looked down at his feet. His shoes were already very small on him. He had blisters on his toes and his feet hurt. "I will make this last pair for myself," he thought, and set to work.

He measured his feet and using his knife carved out soles from the last piece of leather. He worked until late in the afternoon. At last the shoes were ready.

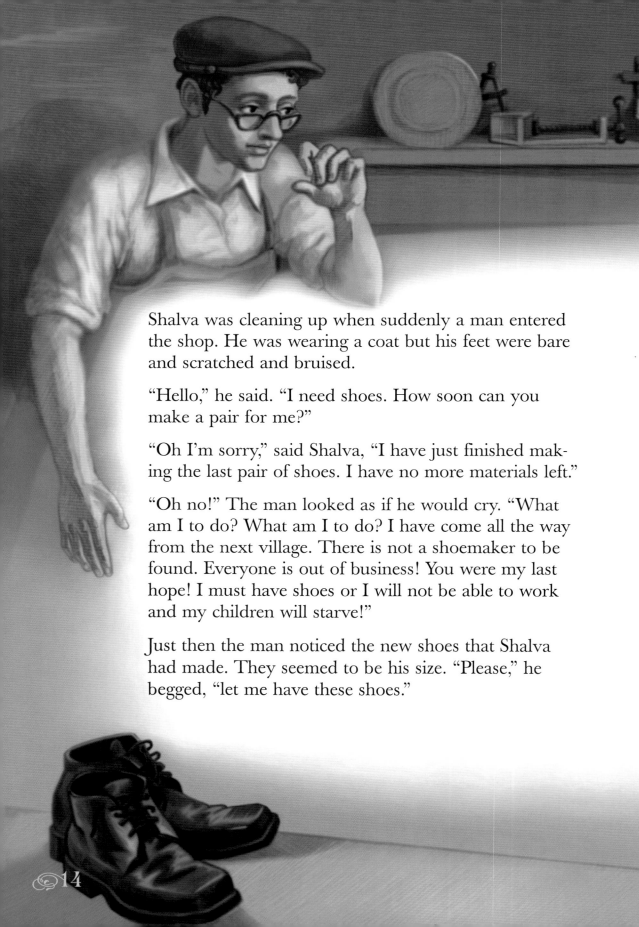

Shalva was cleaning up when suddenly a man entered the shop. He was wearing a coat but his feet were bare and scratched and bruised.

"Hello," he said. "I need shoes. How soon can you make a pair for me?"

"Oh I'm sorry," said Shalva, "I have just finished making the last pair of shoes. I have no more materials left."

"Oh no!" The man looked as if he would cry. "What am I to do? What am I to do? I have come all the way from the next village. There is not a shoemaker to be found. Everyone is out of business! You were my last hope! I must have shoes or I will not be able to work and my children will starve!"

Just then the man noticed the new shoes that Shalva had made. They seemed to be his size. "Please," he begged, "let me have these shoes."

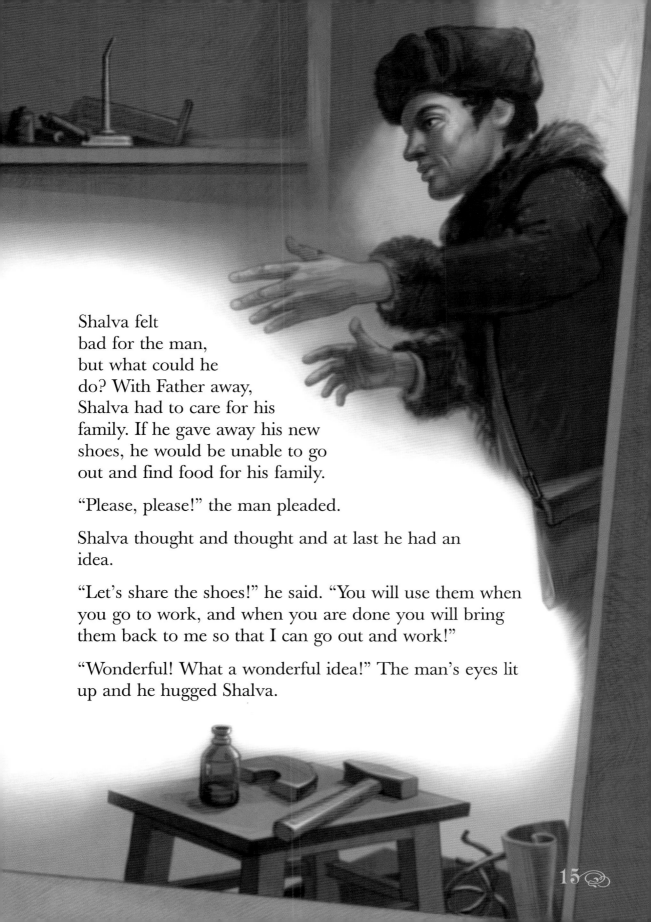

Shalva felt
bad for the man,
but what could he
do? With Father away,
Shalva had to care for his
family. If he gave away his new
shoes, he would be unable to go
out and find food for his family.

"Please, please!" the man pleaded.

Shalva thought and thought and at last he had an idea.

"Let's share the shoes!" he said. "You will use them when you go to work, and when you are done you will bring them back to me so that I can go out and work!"

"Wonderful! What a wonderful idea!" The man's eyes lit up and he hugged Shalva.

"I work in the evening and during the night. I have to go into the forest to collect wood for heating ovens. It is dangerous, and my feet are cut on the thorns and branches.

"The hardest part is when I have to stand on the icy river-bank at the edge of the forest to chop wood. There are a lot of trees there but without shoes there is no way I can stand on the frozen ice. Now I will be able to continue working. Every morning after I sell the wood I will return the shoes to you so that you can go out too."

Shalva was glad that he found a way to help the man. He
cheerfully took the new shoes and gave them to the man.
The man slipped his sore feet into them. They felt smooth
and warm on his cold feet and they fit perfectly. "Thank
you! Thank you!" he cried. "I will bring them back in the
morning," he called as he left the shop.

For many, many months Shalva and the man shared the shoes. The man used them by night, and Shalva wore them during the day. Since he could not make any more new shoes, Shalva took his tools and went from house to house, mending people's shoes as best as he could.

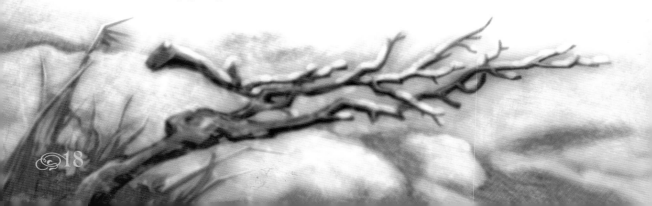

At long last, the war ended. Sadly, Shalva's father did not return home, and no one knew what had happened to him. Shalva had to continue caring for his family.

One morning the man did not come with the shoes. Shalva waited all day and began to worry. He hoped that nothing terrible had happened. A second day passed and a third and still the man did not come.

Shalva was stuck at home. It was chilly and rainy and there were puddles all over the streets. He needed his shoes! By the fourth day Shalva decided to go to work barefoot. He could not stay home waiting forever! Then, just as he was leaving his house, he saw the man approaching.

"Where have you been?" Shalva asked.

The man smiled. "I wanted to repay your kindness to me, so I traveled to the big city and bought some leather for you. It is here in this package," he said, pointing to the bundle on his shoulder. "Now you can start making shoes again!"

Shalva was so excited. He hurried into his shop with the man. Together they opened the package. There was enough leather to make plenty of shoes. Shalva went right to work.

"You can have your shoes back," said the man. "I will buy a new pair now. You really saved my family by sharing your last pair of shoes with me. I don't know what would have happened to us if you hadn't been so kind."

The man returned the shoes, and Shalva made a brand new pair for him. Then he blessed Shalva and left.

"Wow! What a lovely story!" I said when Shalva finished his tale. "Are you still friends with that man?" I asked.

"I never saw him again. Why would I?" Shalva laughed. "I never see any of my customers again. The shoes I make last forever!"

"Really? Do you still have the shoes that you shared with him?"

"Sure!" Shalva smiled. He pointed to his feet. "They are old and out of style but they are strong shoes and I have never stopped wearing them.

"I keep them," he added softly with a twinkle in his eyes, "to remind myself that you can never be too poor to help someone else in need."